CLUE ME IN!

CLUE ME IN!

The Detective Work of
Ethan Flask and Professor von Offel

MAD SCIENCE

by Kathy Burkett
Creative development by Gordon Korman

SCHOLASTIC INC.
New York   Toronto   London   Auckland   Sydney
Mexico City   New Delhi   Hong Kong

ISBN 0-439-22860-3

MAD SCIENCE is a registered trademark of the Mad Science Group used under license by Scholastic Inc.

SCHOLASTIC and associated logos are trademarks and/or registered trademarks of Scholastic Inc.

12 11 10 9 8 7 6 5 4 3 2 1   1 2 3 4 5 6/0
                                           40
Printed in the U.S.A.

First Scholastic printing, February 2001

Table of Contents

Prologue

For more than 100 years, the Flasks, the town of Arcana's first family of science, have been methodically, precisely, safely, *scientifically* inventing all kinds of things.

For more than 100 years, the von Offels, Arcana's first family of sneaks, have been stealing those inventions.

Where the Flasks are brilliant, rational, and reliable, the von Offels are brilliant, reckless, and ruthless. The nearly fabulous Flasks could have earned themselves a major chapter in the history of science — but at every key moment, there always seemed to be a von Offel on the scene to "borrow" a science notebook, beat a Flask to the punch on a patent, or booby-trap an important experiment. Just take a look at the Flask family tree and then at the von Offel clan's tree. Coincidence? Or *evidence*!

Despite being tricked out of fame and fortune by the awful von Offels, the Flasks doggedly continued their scientific inquiries. The last of the family line, Ethan Flask, is no exception. An outstanding sixth-grade science teacher, he's also conducting studies into animal intelligence and is competing for the Third Millennium Foundation's prestigious Vanguard Teacher Award. Unfortunately, the person who's evaluating Ethan for the award is none other than Professor John von Offel, a.k.a. the original mad scientist, Johannes von Offel. Von Offel needs a Flask to help him regain the body he lost in an explosive experiment many decades ago. When last seen in *Watch Out! The Daring Disasters of Ethan Flask and Professor von Offel*, the professor caused a whirlwind of chaos at Einstein Elementary School.

Now von Offel is beginning to look suspiciously like the source of all the other wacky mishaps that have hit the school lately. The school principal is worried. The PTA wants the police called in. The professor's got to deflect some of that unwanted attention. So, like a true von Offel, he shifts the blame — to a Flask!

You'll find step-by-step instructions for the experiment mentioned on page 35 of this book in *Detective and Spy Science,* the Mad Science experiments log.

The Nearly Fabulous Flasks

Jedidiah Flask
2nd person to create rubber band

Oliver Flask
Missed appointment to patent new glue because he was mysteriously epoxied to his chair

Augustus Flask
Developed telephone; got a busy signal

Mildred Flask Tachyon
Tranquilizer formula never registered; carriage horses fell asleep en route to patent office

Percy Flask
Lost notes on cure for common cold in pick-pocketing incident

Lane Tachyon
Developed laughing gas; was kept in hysterics while a burglar stole the formula

Archibald Flask
Knocked out cold en route to patent superior baseball bat

Marlow Flask
Runner-up to Adolphus von Offel for Sir Isaac Newton Science Prize

Amaryllis Flask Lepton
Discovered new kind of amoeba; never published findings due to dysentery

Norton Flask
Clubbed with an overcooked meat loaf and robbed of prototype microwave oven

Salome Flask Rhombus
Discovered cloud-salting with dry ice; never made it to patent office due to freak downpour

Roland Flask
His new high-speed engine was believed to have powered the getaway car that stole his prototype

Constance Rhombus Ampère
Lost Marie Curie award to Beatrice O'Door; voted Miss Congeniality

Margaret Flask Geiger
Name was mysteriously deleted from registration papers for her undetectable correction fluid

Michael Flask
Arrived with gas grill schematic only to find tailgate party outside patent office

Solomon Ampère
Bionic horse placed in Kentucky Derby after von Offel entry

Ethan Flask

The Awful von Offels

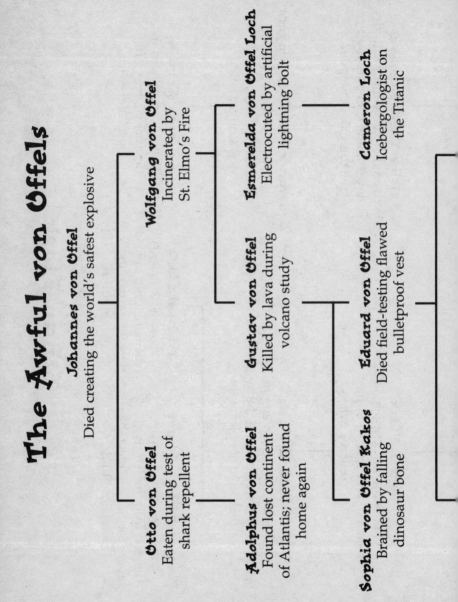

Johannes von Offel
Died creating the world's safest explosive

Wolfgang von Offel
Incinerated by
St. Elmo's Fire

Esmerelda von Offel Loch
Electrocuted by artificial
lightning bolt

Cameron Loch
Icebergologist on
the Titanic

Gustav von Offel
Killed by lava during
volcano study

Eduard von Offel
Died field-testing flawed
bulletproof vest

Otto von Offel
Eaten during test of
shark repellent

Adolphus von Offel
Found lost continent
of Atlantis; never found
home again

Sophia von Offel Kakos
Brained by falling
dinosaur bone

Rula von Offel Malle
Evaporated

Beatrice Malle O'Door
Drowned pursuing the
Loch Ness Monster

Kurt von Offel
Weak batteries in
antigravity backpack

Colin von Offel
Transplanted his brain
into wildebeest

Feldspar O'Door
Died of freezer burn
during cryogenics
experiment

Alan von Offel
Failed to survive field
test of nonpoisonous
arsenic

Felicity von Offel Day
Brained by diving bell
during deep-sea
exploration

Professor John von Offel (?)

Johannes von Offel's
Book of Scientific Observations, 1891

Jedidiah Flask has been spying on me. It is not my imagination. Who would be better equipped to recognize the signs than I, who have been spying on him for the better part of a generation? Most recently, I have pirated his supersecret hair restorer. By adding a few additional key ingredients, I have converted it into an extremely powerful glue. I'm not sure if Jedidiah has noticed yet. Come to think of it, he has been wearing the same fur hat since February, which must be uncomfortable as we head into the dog days of summer. All the same, I think I shall call the police and have him arrested. If I allow his espionage to go unpunished, that might seriously cut down on the amount of time I'll be able to spend spying on him . . .

CHAPTER 1

Man's Best Friend?

The pedestrian signal turned to WALK. Alberta Wong, Luis Antilla, and Prescott Forrester were about to step into the crosswalk.

"Watch out! Coming through!" a voice rang out. A blurry figure flashed an arm's length in front of them, then disappeared around a corner.

The sixth graders hopped back onto the sidewalk.

"Was that Mr. Flask?" Alberta asked.

"It sounded like him," Prescott said. "But whoever it was was rushing *away* from school."

"Let's check it out." Luis sprinted around the corner.

Resting on the curb was science teacher Ethan Flask, in a helmet and pads; a skateboard lay at his side.

"So that *was* you, Mr. Flask," Luis said.

The science teacher smiled sheepishly. "Sorry. I know I should have stopped when the light turned, but I lost control of things for a minute — or should I say I lost control of *him*." Mr. Flask struggled with a large golden retriever, who was bounding playfully at the end of a leash.

Alberta approached the dog and held out her hand, palm up. The retriever sniffed, then gave Alberta's fingers a big, juicy lick. He jumped up and tried to lick her face.

"Sit, boy!" Mr. Flask commanded. He held his hand in front of the retriever's face. The dog pranced from side to side for a moment, then sat down. "Good dog! Now I can make proper introductions. Meet Alberta, Luis, and Prescott. Guys, this is Edgar."

Edgar jumped up at the sound of his name. Mr. Flask held out his hand again. "Sit, boy." The dog cocked his head, tongue hanging out. Mr. Flask pushed down on Edgar's rear quarters. They didn't budge. He pushed harder. "Dogs are famous for being both intelligent and trainable," he grunted. "So I figured a dog would be a natural subject for my ongoing study of animal intelligence." Mr. Flask gritted his teeth and pushed even harder, and Edgar's tail finally touched the ground. "Good boy," the teacher said.

Luis patted Edgar's back. "What are you trying to train him to do? Work with blind people? Find people buried by earthquakes? Deliver and retrieve important messages?"

Mr. Flask shook his head. "Right now I'd settle for being able to stop him from taking things and burying them. Edgar disappeared with my best microscope yesterday. I've searched half the town for it, and I still have no clue where he might have hidden it!"

As if on cue, Edgar jumped up and yanked a piece of paper out of Prescott's hand. Then he darted down the street, easily tearing away from Mr. Flask's grip.

"Edgar!" Mr. Flask yelled. He ran after the dog, trying to grab hold of his leash. Luis, Alberta, and Prescott raced after their teacher. Four blocks later, Mr. Flask slowed to a halt. The others caught up with him. "It's no use," Mr. Flask said. "We won't catch up with Edgar until he wants us to. And by then that paper will be buried and gone. I hope it wasn't an important homework assignment, Prescott."

Prescott blushed and bit his lip. "English," he said.

"I'll write you a note," Mr. Flask said. He shook his head, then laughed. "Ms. Patel should enjoy that one! 'Please excuse Prescott. A dog buried his homework.'"

Just then, a sporty red car pulled up to the curb. The driver rolled down her window.

"Hello, Dr. Kepler," Alberta said. "The funniest thing just happened —"

"Shhhh," Luis hissed.

"I'd love to hear your story later, Alberta," Dr.

Kepler said. "But right now I need to speak to your teacher before school begins. Ethan, why don't you hop in, and we'll talk on the way."

Mr. Flask looked at the lab assistants.

"We'll find Edgar," Luis said.

"And pick up your skateboard," Prescott added.

Mr. Flask nodded. He ran around to the passenger side and hopped into the principal's car.

Luis turned to Alberta. "Some things a principal doesn't have to know," he said.

"You don't volunteer in the office like I do," Alberta said. "Dr. Kepler has a very good sense of humor."

The principal's car pulled away. "I'm afraid this is no longer funny," Dr. Kepler said to Mr. Flask. "I've been receiving a growing number of phone calls from parents about the bizarre mishaps taking place at Einstein Elementary. Mrs. Ratner and the other PTA officers are even calling for a police investigation."

"There have definitely been some strange events since the professor came," Mr. Flask agreed. "But I can't say that any real crimes have been committed. Just weird stuff like exploding watermelons and spontaneous tornadoes."

"Weird indeed," said Dr. Kepler. "At this point, I'm at a loss as to what to do. Do you really think that Professor von Offel might be involved somehow?"

Mr. Flask thought for a moment. "I can't help

4

suspecting the professor," he began. "Whenever something strange happens, he always seems to be in the middle of it. On the other hand, there's been a long history of feuding between my family and his. I heard a lot of awful von Offel stories growing up, so I can't rule out the possibility that my judgment is a bit clouded. Anyway, at this point, I don't think anyone without our inside knowledge would suspect the professor. After all, he's a representative of the prestigious Third Millennium Foundation. Plus he's a descendent of a prominent local family."

Dr. Kepler cleared her throat carefully. "I was thinking more along the lines of what to do if the parents should suspect *you*."

"Suspect me?" Mr. Flask's eyes grew wide. "Who in the world could possibly suspect me?"

The school custodian had a police officer cornered in the hallway.

"Ethan Flask is behind it all," Mr. Klumpp said. "I'll bet my reputation as a custodian on it."

Detective Robert Shapiro nodded politely. "You understand that I'm only here to do a Community Safety Day presentation, right?"

Mr. Klumpp shook his head impatiently. "It's community safety that's at risk, Detective! Tornadoes in the basement, wild apes running amok, exploding fruit . . ."

"As this town's newest police detective, I take your charges very seriously," Detective Shapiro interrupted. "According to the *Arcana Detective Handbook*, every crime brought to the attention of the police must be investigated. However, so far nothing you've described to me is a crime. Nobody got hurt. No school property was stolen or damaged."

"Isn't disorder a crime of its own?" Mr. Klumpp asked. "Flask has been nothing but trouble since the day he was hired. I've spent more time cleaning up his lab after some cockamamy experiment than all the other classrooms combined!"

"Under the circumstances, I can't arrest someone just for making a mess," the detective said. "I'm sorry. The rules are very clear. Until I have an official crime report, I can't investigate this science teacher or anyone else. Now, if you had any evidence that Flask was involved in criminal activities, *that* would be different."

Mr. Klumpp sniffed defiantly. "Since you're new to detective work, you may not realize that custodians are the eyes and ears of a school. When I find evidence fingering Ethan Flask — and I will find it — I'll report it to your superior."

Detective Shapiro sighed. "There's no need for that, Mr. Klumpp. I'm not writing off your concerns. I just need some proof of a crime — and reasonable suspicion that Flask is involved."

"Then question Flask yourself," the custodian said. "You're visiting the school, so talk to the teachers. What could be more natural?"

The detective pulled a copy of the *Arcana Detective Handbook* out of his back pocket. He thumbed through it, nodded, then put it away. "All right, Mr. Klumpp. Looks like I can comply with that request. I'll find some excuse to stop by Flask's classroom. But to do anything more, I'm sure I'll need evidence."

"No problem," Mr. Klumpp said. "I'm certain the equipment associated with every single bizarre occurrence can be traced to the sixth-grade science lab." He smiled and leaned closer to Detective Shapiro. "You know, custodians are no strangers to detective work. It's amazing what you find out about people when it's your job to empty their garbage."

CHAPTER 2

Edgar Unleashed

" **I** n you go," said Alberta. She tugged on Edgar's collar as Prescott opened the door to the sixth-grade lab. Luis stood behind the dog, blocking his escape.

"Edgar! Here, boy," said Mr. Flask. The golden retriever wandered right into the classroom, stopping to sniff palms and lick sneakers. He was quickly surrounded by sixth graders.

Mr. Flask looked on a little nervously. "Guys, you can pet Edgar all you like," he said. "Just keep an eye on your personal belongings, okay? And Sean, no junk-food dog treats, please."

"Who, me?" Sean Baxter smiled and wiped orange crumbs from Edgar's hairy lips.

Professor John von Offel swept into the room, followed by his parrot, Atom. He cast a quick glance at Edgar. "I thought this was a science laboratory, Flask, not a petting zoo."

Luis leaned toward Prescott and Alberta. "Considering he takes that parrot with him wherever he goes . . ."

Alberta smiled. "He doesn't mean anything by those comments. I think he just likes to project the image of a crusty old genius."

"Since he can't even fully project his own shadow, you'd think he'd keep his mouth shut," Prescott said.

Mr. Flask took the dog by the collar. "Edgar is part of my ongoing work with animal intelligence, Professor. I bring in my lab animals because I find that students really respond to them. It's part of my —"

"Yes, yes, your plan to increase student interest in science," the professor said. "I get it, Flask. I get it." He adjusted his monocle. "Now, in my day, all a student needed for science exploration was a scrap of wool and a glass rod. But if you really think that in order to get the attention of youngsters today, you have to coddle them, and pet them, and practically slobber all over them —"

Suddenly, Edgar lurched forward, pulling away from Mr. Flask. He bounded to the back of the classroom, stuck his muzzle into the professor's face, and picked off the old man's monocle with a juicy flick of his tongue. Then he made for the open door.

"Stop that canine!" the professor shouted.

Mr. Flask dived for Edgar. He caught the monocle but was unable to yank it out of Edgar's jaws.

"Do something," the professor hissed at Atom. The bird took off into the air and dive-bombed Edgar, but he bounced off the dog's back like a

Ping-Pong ball. Edgar twisted free of Mr. Flask's grip and bolted out the door.

Mr. Flask scrambled to the doorway, but by then Edgar was nowhere to be seen. He turned back to the professor and shook his head. "It's no use. Edgar is a compulsive burier. We may never get your monocle back."

The professor scowled. "That certainly makes it difficult for me to write my report for the foundation, doesn't it?"

The teacher forced himself to smile. "I'll do everything in my power to find your monocle, Professor. Hopefully, while I'm at it, I'll find my microscope."

"And my English report," Prescott added.

Edgar came bounding back into the classroom, a satisfied look on his face. Mr. Flask caught him by the collar and led him back to a large dog bed in the corner of the classroom. "Sit, boy," he commanded. Edgar sat and scratched his ear lazily. "Now, lie down." Edgar yawned and lowered himself onto the bed. "Good boy. Now stay." Edgar closed his eyes. By the time Mr. Flask returned to the front of the classroom, Edgar was already snoring.

"Mr. Flask?" Detective Shapiro stood at the door, looking over the classroom.

"I'm Ethan Flask."

The officer held out his hand. "Detective Shapiro. I'm giving the Community Safety Day presentation today. I'm early, so I thought I'd stop by some classrooms — at random, of course — and try to get to know my audience."

Mr. Flask motioned for the officer to come in. "Great! This is a sixth-grade science class. I'm sure they'd be very interested to hear about your work. After all, scientists and detectives have a lot in common. Class, any ideas about how the two are alike?"

Alberta raised her hand. "They both search for clues that can help them find the truth?"

Detective Shapiro nodded. Mr. Flask smiled.

"They both have to think very logically," Luis added. "They can't let their feelings get in the way."

"Scientists can't be so attached to a theory that they can't question it," Mr. Flask agreed.

"Detectives have to suspect everyone," Detective Shapiro added. "Sometimes the most charming and likable people end up being the criminals."

Mr. Flask turned toward the officer. "How do detectives know where to begin an investigation? Scientists have to start with what can be easily observed and what others have discovered."

"Again, that's a lot like detective work." Detective Shapiro pulled out his notebook. "It would be easier if we took an example. Has anything *unexplained* happened around Einstein Elementary this year?"

"Detective Shapeeer-o," Max Hoof called out. "During our costume dance, the gymnasium filled with a stinky mist. My mother thinks it injured my

11

sinuses. I didn't get any nosebleeds for an entire week afterward."

Atom fluttered up onto the professor's shoulder. "Looks like the jig is up," he whispered.

"Nonsense," the professor hissed. His expression suggested boredom, but Atom noticed that his knuckles were white with tension.

Heather Patterson's manicured hand shot up. "My father was at a PTA meeting, and a huge watermelon exploded."

"Hoo, boy," Atom muttered. The professor snatched the bird off his shoulder and plopped him back on his brass perch.

"But the best was when that ape went berserk during the book fair," Sean Baxter said. "Unless — Mr. Flask, is it true that there was a tornado in the basement?"

Detective Shapiro's pen hovered over his note-book. He raised his eyebrows and looked at Mr. Flask.

The teacher smiled and shrugged. "I guess we've had a very unusual year."

The detective turned back to the class. "Suppose I was investigating these incidents. First I would get all the details — eyewitness accounts, any physical evidence . . ."

"My father's tie still has pink stains on it," Heather offered.

Detective Shapiro nodded. "Yes, that kind of

thing. Then I would look to see if anything linked the events together."

"How would you do that?" Heather asked.

"Well, I might pick a person and see whether the events all related to him or her." Detective Shapiro put his finger to his mouth thoughtfully. "Just as an example — is each of these events connected in any way to Mr. Flask here?"

The teacher's smile froze as he thought about his earlier conversation with Dr. Kepler. He looked at Detective Shapiro, but the officer avoided his gaze.

Sean raised his hand. "Well, that wacko ape belonged to Mr. Flask."

"My dad said the watermelon exploded while Mr. Flask's lab assistants were performing," Heather said.

"And the green mist appeared when Mr. Flask was onstage," Max added.

The professor smiled and poked Atom with his quill pen. "What did I say?" he whispered.

Luis narrowed his eyes. Why was the detective writing these silly coincidences in his notebook? He raised his hand. "None of that proves anything," he said.

Detective Shapiro smiled, but not warmly. "Of course not," he replied. "It's just a collection of very interesting facts. And anyway, as far as I know, none of those incidents involved crimes — unless anyone can tell me otherwise?" He paused and waited for the class's reaction.

Luis looked at Alberta, eyebrows raised.

Alberta thought for a moment and raised her hand. "Don't detectives have to be very observant, Detective Shapiro? Maybe you could give us some tips on observation."

The detective nodded. "The key is to notice as much detail as possible, because you never know what will later prove to be important. For instance, when I came in today I immediately noticed a large golden retriever sleeping in the back. Of course, anyone would notice that because it's so unusual — almost unheard of — in an elementary school classroom."

Mr. Flask opened his mouth to speak, then closed it again.

"However, as a detective," Shapiro continued, "I couldn't stop there. I automatically looked to see whether he had the right dog tags. It appears he does. I also noted whether he was on a leash, which he was not. I made a mental note — that may be a violation of Arcana's leash law. We're not outside, but we are on public property, so I'd have to check."

Sean laughed. "Could you really arrest Mr. Flask for having an unleashed dog in class?"

"Probably not on the first offense," Detective Shapiro said seriously. "If it is a violation, though, he might have to pay a fine."

The professor scribbled furiously. "I expect you to follow up on this, Flask," he said. "The Third Millennium Foundation does not condone lawlessness."

Mr. Flask looked a bit dazed. "Of course," he said. "In the meantime, I suppose I should put a leash on him, just to be sure." He reached behind his desk for Edgar's chain and walked toward the back. As soon as the dog heard the metal links clinking together, he stirred. When he saw Mr. Flask approaching with the leash, he immediately took off. He swerved around the teacher and trotted to the front of the classroom. When he reached Detective Shapiro, the retriever jumped up on his hind legs, grabbed the detective's notebook in his teeth, and bolted out the door.

"Edgar! Come, boy!" Mr. Flask shouted as he ran toward the doorway. The dog kept running, with Detective Shapiro in hot pursuit. Quickly, the action moved to the school yard. The class watched through the windows as the dog and the detective ran in and out of view. Edgar zigzagged around the school yard. He would stop, turn playfully toward Detective Shapiro, then bound away as soon as the officer approached. Both disappeared around the corner for a few minutes. Then Edgar tore across the school yard alone. A moment later, Detective Shapiro ran the same path, panting heavily. Finally, Detective Shapiro reappeared at the science lab door, holding Edgar by the collar.

Mr. Flask led dog to the back of the room and

chained him up. When he turned, Detective Shapiro was removing a booklet from his pocket.

"Oh, you got your detective notebook back!" Mr. Flask said. "That's a relief. I'm really sorry about Edgar. I'm afraid his training isn't going so well."

Detective Shapiro's pen moved over the booklet. "This isn't . . . my notebook," he said, his breathing still heavy. "I'm writing you . . . a ticket. I don't know . . . whether your dog . . . has to be leashed . . . in your classroom . . . but I'm certain . . . he should be leashed . . . outside."

The detective ripped out the ticket and handed it to Mr. Flask. Then he turned to the class. "See you all . . . at the Community Safety Day . . . presentation."

Mr. Flask tucked the ticket into his pocket. He forced a smile. "I understand, Detective. You have to do your duty." He cleared his throat. "Thank you for stopping by and telling us about detective work. Class, let's show Detective Shapiro our appreciation."

The applause was uneven. The lab assistants were too stunned to clap at all. But Sean was clapping wildly and whistling loudly. "Yo! Speedy Shapiro!" he called out.

Detective Shapiro waved briefly and walked out.

Mr. Flask turned toward the class. Now his smile was genuine. "Well, that was unexpected, but very interesting. This seems to me like a perfect beginning for a unit on detective science."

CHAPTER 3

A One-Bird Crime Wave

After class, the professor returned to his office with Atom.

"You know," the professor said, "maybe this Flask has some von Offel blood in him after all. Being in trouble with the law is one of our proud family traditions."

Atom laughed. "But in this case, Flask is actually innocent."

The professor smiled. "Guilty, innocent, what's the difference? As long as they suspect *him* and not me."

"Detective Shapiro seemed pretty sharp," Atom said. "Aren't you even a little afraid he'll figure out you're behind all the craziness at this school?"

The professor shook his head. "Not as long as I follow the von Offel creed: 'Always be as erratic as possible. Then no rational person can pin anything on you.'"

"That explains a lot," Atom said. "I'm guessing you wrote that creed yourself?"

The professor nodded proudly. "I am the original von Offel, after all."

Atom shook his head. "On another subject, what are you going to do without your monocle?"

"Oh, I don't even need it!" the professor scoffed. "I only wear it because it makes me look so distinguished." He nudged the parrot with his elbow. "All the ladies love a monocle, eh? But not every man can carry one off."

"You do have a . . . *unique* look," Atom said. "But are you sure you don't need your monocle? Didn't you accidentally stumble into the supply closet on the way over here?"

"That was no accident," Professor von Offel insisted. "I was checking on Flask's supplies. A good teacher stays well stocked. So naturally I have to check supplies as part of my report to the Third Millennium Foundation."

The bird looked skeptical. "You're putting *paper towels* in your report about Flask's teaching?"

"Expect it to be a highlight." The professor leaned back in his chair and put his feet on his desk. "So far I have nothing else to say. Flask keeps experimenting and experimenting, but he still hasn't found a way to bring me a hundred percent back to life."

Atom rolled his eyes. "Not only is that not in his job description, he doesn't even know you want it done!"

The professor yawned. "Excuses, excuses." His eyes closed. After a moment, he was snoring softly.

Atom fluttered down to the floor. Each time the professor exhaled, his body sank until the seat of his pants sagged below the wooden seat. Then the professor would inhale, and his body would rise to the surface again.

"Amazing," Atom chuckled to himself. "I never get tired of watching that."

Outside von Offel's office, Mr. Flask's sixth graders noisily filed by, heading down the hall to the gymnasium for the Community Safety Day presentation.

"The science lab will be empty," Atom mused. "Sounds like an opportunity Johannes wouldn't want to miss." He nudged the professor with his wing.

"Keep your feathers off me," the professor mumbled sleepily. "Or I'll teach you the true meaning of extra crispy."

The noise outside had stopped. Atom inched open the door and peeked out at the empty hallway. "Well, someone has to take some action," he said. He fluttered down the hall and ducked into the science lab.

Atom circled around the room, buzzing a hairbreadth from the sleeping Edgar. He landed on Mr. Flask's desk, which was covered with batteries, lightbulbs, and wires.

The bird lifted a lightbulb thoughtfully. "If the professor saw this stuff, he'd get a flash of inspiration for some kind of invention." He chuckled. "It'd be a ridiculous invention that would probably be a spectacular failure. But it *would* be inspired. That's one thing I can't help him with." He tossed the bulb back into the pile.

Just then, the door handle turned. Atom quickly fluttered down and hid behind the desk.

Mr. Flask burst into the room. "Great news, Edgar! Dr. Kepler called the sheriff, and you don't need a leash inside the classroom." Edgar lifted his head sleepily. The teacher unclipped the leash and tossed it aside. Then he scratched Edgar behind the ears. "We're lucky enough to have a principal who once competed in the Iditarod dogsled race." He turned Edgar's face to his. "She loves dogs, but let's not push it. You've got to shape up and stop grabbing stuff, okay?"

Edgar licked the teacher's face.

"I'll take that as a yes," Mr. Flask said. "At least it better be." He stood up and headed for the door. "Well, back to the Community Safety Day presentation." He headed into the hallway. He didn't notice that he'd left the door slightly ajar behind him.

Atom fluttered back up to the top of the desk. Edgar walked aimlessly around, sniffing. Many of the sixth graders had left their backpacks in the science lab rather than lug them to the gym for the presentation. Edgar stopped at Sean's desk. His backpack had a large grease stain on the bottom, and it smelled like beef jerky. Edgar scratched at the backpack and whined.

Atom hopped across the desks and looked at the dog. "I bet you're wishing you had opposable thumbs right about now," he said. "Well, I've got the next best thing — claws." Atom stepped on top of the backpack and unzipped it. Then he hopped inside, rustled around some paper bags, and came up with a half-eaten stick of beef jerky. He tossed it to Edgar, who swallowed it eagerly. Atom rustled around some more and threw Edgar some potato chips. Edgar licked them off the ground but looked less satisfied. He wandered over to Heather's desk.

Atom zipped up Sean's backpack, then joined Edgar at Heather's desk. "You're going to get Flask into a lot of trouble someday," he said to Edgar. The dog smiled, then sniffed Heather's backpack. "I think Flask might finally have slipped up in his study of animal intelligence," Atom continued. "Most dogs are pretty smart. But you seem a few biscuits short of a box." Edgar licked Heather's backpack.

"Okay, let's see what's in here." Atom pulled out a plastic container. "Nothing but a health salad, an apple, some carrots and celery." Edgar sniffed the food, then backed away. Atom dropped the container into the backpack. He started to zip it up again, but Edgar nosed him out of the way. The dog stuck his head down into the backpack and pulled

21

out a Walkman. He bolted for the partly open door, pried it open with his paw, and took off down the hallway.

"Oops! Luckily, no one will ever guess how that Walkman walked away." Atom zipped up Heather's backpack. Then he chuckled. "In fact, that detective will probably suspect Flask. Hmm. More blame cast on Flask means less on the professor." Atom flew to the window and watched as Edgar buried the Walkman. "I think I just found a way to help Johannes."

A few minutes later, Edgar returned. He poked his head into the classroom, sniffed the air, then walked down the hall. Atom took off after him. "Good dog," the bird said. "Let's see what else we can dig up."

CHAPTER 4

Definitely in the Deceptive Range

Prescott plopped down next to Luis and Alberta and opened his bag lunch. "I just saw Detective Shapiro in the hallway," he said.

Alberta put down her sandwich. "But the whole school saw his presentation yesterday. What could he be doing here today?"

"Maybe he decided he *should* investigate all of the weird stuff that's been going on around here," Luis said. "The problem is, he seems to suspect Mr. Flask."

"So let's tell him about the professor," Prescott said. "We have enough evidence on him to prove that he's a ghost and that all of those strange things are his fault."

Luis shook his head. "We don't have *evidence*. Just stuff we've seen — our own observations. And we can't exactly tell Detective Shapiro that we saw the professor walk through a train. He'd never believe us."

"I'm not sure I'd want him to," Alberta said.

"Whatever else Professor von Offel is, he's Mr. Flask's observer for the Vanguard Teacher Award."

"The foundation could send a replacement," Prescott suggested.

Alberta shook her head. "Even if they did, it would look bad for Mr. Flask. There's no way he would win the award after that."

"Well, at least he wouldn't lose his job," Prescott said, "which he might if the detective convinces Dr. Kepler that Mr. Flask is behind all of those weird events."

Alberta thought for a minute. "If Detective Shapiro really starts focusing on Mr. Flask, we'll look for evidence against the professor. But until then, let's just wait and see. The best thing would be if he just let the whole thing drop."

The lab assistants got to science class just before the bell rang. Detective Shapiro was there talking to Mr. Flask.

"They're smiling," Alberta whispered. "That's a good sign."

"We'll see," Prescott said. "Remember, the detective says that he doesn't let his personal feelings get in the way of an investigation."

As the bell rang, the professor and Atom sailed into class. Edgar sprang up from his dog bed and trotted over to the professor's desk. He nosed Atom eagerly. The parrot tried to ignore him.

"That's weird," Luis whispered. "All the other classroom animals *hate* Atom."

Mr. Flask led Edgar back to his dog bed and convinced him to lie down. "Edgar and I worked a few bugs out of his training last night," Mr. Flask said. "But just in case, I'll close the door."

The detective nodded.

"Class, I invited Detective Shapiro back today as part of our detective science unit," Mr. Flask said. "I thought he might help us build burglar alarms, but he's brought something even more exciting. Detective?"

"Yes, I thought your class might be interested to see how a polygraph machine — also called a lie detector — works." The detective motioned toward a laptop computer attached to some wires. "Mr. Flask, will you be my first subject?"

The teacher sat down next to the polygraph.

"A polygraph measures three body functions," Detective Shapiro said. He attached two tubes to Mr. Flask's torso. "This measures breathing." He slipped a thick cuff on Mr. Flask's upper arm. "Blood pressure," he explained. Then he attached metal plates to two of the teacher's fingers. "These monitor sweat by measuring how well the skin conducts electricity. The more sweat, the better the conductivity."

"Breathing rate, blood pressure, and sweat all increase when a person is nervous," he continued.

"Because of that, they're also a good measure of whether someone is lying." He turned to Mr. Flask. "Relax, and the polygraph will measure your normal readings."

"Detective Shapeer-o!" Max called out. "What if your normal readings show you're always pretty nervous?"

"That's why we take a base reading," the detective said. "Some people start lower, and some start higher. The important thing is how much the readings change. Besides, a good polygraph operator relaxes the subject by explaining the machinery and reviewing the questions ahead of time. Today, we're working a little more on the fly."

Detective Shapiro turned back to Mr. Flask. "Let's think of an interesting topic to interview you about."

"How about what questions are on the next quiz?" Sean called out.

Mr. Flask laughed. "This isn't truth serum, Sean. You'll have to wait until I pass out the test papers."

The detective glanced at his computer screen. "I'm not an *expert* polygraph reader, but that looked like a *nondeceptive*, or truthful, answer." He turned back to Mr. Flask. "Anyway, I thought it might be fun to ask you about some of the unexplained events the students mentioned yesterday."

"What did I say?" Prescott whispered. "He's still after Mr. Flask!"

Alberta bit her lip.

"That's interesting," the detective noted. "I already see some increase in these readings." He looked at the teacher curiously. "Anyway, before we begin, I need to see what your readings look like when you're being deceptive. Tell me a lie."

Mr. Flask laughed. "Teachers never lie."

Detective Shapiro checked his screen. "That'll do fine. Now for some questions. Were your lab assistants performing for the PTA when the watermelon exploded?"

"Yes, they were," Mr. Flask said.

"Was this the same week you were promoting explosions in your classroom?"

Mr. Flask looked flustered. "No. I mean, I wasn't *promoting* them. We were studying explosive reactions."

"I see," the detective said. "Did you teach explosions because they are a specific part of some state science curriculum?"

The teacher shook his head. "No. The state curriculum isn't the same as a lesson plan. I teach all the science basics, but I choose the topics based on my students' interests — and mine, of course."

"So you and your students share an interest in explosions?"

Mr. Flask smiled weakly. "Well, don't most people?"

The detective turned toward the class. "Of course, if this were a real investigation, I'd press my subject for a more direct answer."

Mr. Flask laughed. "Then the direct answer would be yes."

"Is it true that your orangutan ran wild during a book fair?"

Mr. Flask was silent for a moment. "I suppose the direct answer would be yes," he said slowly. "But a lot of strange things happened that day."

"And the mist and goop that flooded the gym during the costume dance," the detective said. "Might they have been created using your lab equipment?"

"I suppose . . . that is, yes," Mr. Flask answered.

"Do you have any idea who could be behind all of these strange events, Mr. Flask?"

The teacher gulped. "No."

The detective watched the screen for a second. "Let me ask that one again. Do you have any idea how these strange things happened?"

Mr. Flask turned pale. "No," he repeated.

The detective turned to the class and smiled. "I guess it's a good thing that no crimes were committed, or I'd be hauling your teacher in for more questioning. The readings on his last answer are definitely in the deceptive range."

He unhooked Mr. Flask from the equipment.

"Young man," the professor spoke up. "How reliable is that test?"

"It's not foolproof," Detective Shapiro said. "But when done correctly, a polygraph is a valuable tool for separating truth from lies."

"Indeed." The professor stood up. "Well, I'd like to try it myself."

"Are you nuts?" Atom whispered. The professor shooed the bird off his shoulder and strode to the front of the classroom. "Hook me up."

The detective fitted the equipment on him. He looked at the screen and raised his eyebrows. He fiddled a few connections and checked again. "You must be a very calm person, Professor," he said. "I've never seen such low readings."

"You did say you were new to detective work," the professor noted. "Anyway, why wouldn't I be calm? I'm completely innocent. Go ahead and ask me anything about the recent strange events."

"Okay, do *you* have any idea who's responsible?" Detective Shapiro asked.

"None," the professor laughed. "Though Flask's performance on this contraption does make me suspect *him*."

"His orangutan attacked you, didn't it?" the detective asked.

The professor sniffed. "Yes, and I have no idea why."

"Do you have any knowledge of a tornado in the school basement?" the detective asked.

"None whatsoever," the professor scoffed. "What a ridiculous notion!"

"And do you know anything about this mysterious mist and goo that appeared during the costume dance?"

The professor smiled. "I managed to obtain a sample of the goo, and I put it through some laboratory tests. I found it contained a large volume of corn syrup, water, and gelatin."

Detective Shapiro looked puzzled. "Is that significant?"

"Perhaps," the professor replied. "Those are the ingredients for Mr. Flask's artificial mucus."

Detective Shapiro silently removed the equipment from the professor's body.

Mr. Flask swallowed hard. "Detective, that was another very interesting presentation. Guys, let's give him a hand."

The class was silent. Finally, Mr. Flask began clapping, and a few stunned students joined in.

The detective carried his equipment to the door. "Thank you, Mr. Flask. I think we all learned something today."

When the professor returned to his seat, Atom hopped up on his shoulder.

"Are you crazy?" the bird whispered. "You volunteered for a polygraph test, then lied your head off!"

"Yes," the professor hissed back. "And as a result, all suspicion has been shifted from me and on to Flask."

"But how did you know the polygraph wouldn't catch you?"

The professor casually poked his quill pen

through his forearm, then removed it. "There are *some* benefits to my condition."

Out in the hallway, Mr. Klumpp thrust two mops into the detective's face. "I found you some evidence! This mop has artificial mucus in it. The other one is full of the goop from the costume dance. Take them back to your lab. I bet you'll find they're suspiciously similar."

The detective sighed. "There's no need. I've just seen evidence that suggests the same. But I still haven't uncovered any crime. I'm sorry, Mr. Klumpp, I've done all I can."

The custodian's eyes narrowed. "Well, I haven't!"

Detective Shapiro watched the custodian stomp away angrily.

"Detective!" he heard behind him.

He turned. "Dr. Kepler?"

"I'm so glad to see you." She handed the detective a piece of paper. "I'm afraid we have a thief in this building. All of these items were stolen. I believe it happened during your Community Safety Day presentation."

"A Walkman, a Barbie doll, a handheld power drill, a gelatin mold full of lemon Jell-O," the detective read aloud from the dozen items on the list. "I assume you're going to file a complaint with the police so that I can begin a full investigation?"

Dr. Kepler nodded reluctantly.

"I'll drive you over to the station now, and we can take care of it," he said. They walked toward the exit.

Mr. Klumpp peeked around the corner at the other end of the hall. "That principal can't fool me," he muttered. "She's making up this phantom thief in order to deflect attention from her favorite science teacher! Well, *my* investigation isn't over."

As the last school bus left for the day, the professor and Atom were walking around the school yard with a shovel.

"Where was that blasted dog burying things?" the professor fumed.

Atom looked around nervously. "I wouldn't know, of course."

"I want that monocle back — for sentimental reasons only, of course. Hmmm. This soil looks disturbed." The professor jabbed the shovel into the ground. He tossed aside a few shovelfuls of dirt and pulled out a book. He brushed it off. "The detective's notebook," he said thoughtfully. Then he tossed it back into the hole and covered it with dirt.

"What are you doing?" Atom asked.

The professor smiled. "It's entertaining to watch young Flask squirm. But I can't risk the police gathering too many facts — and getting too close to the true source of the disruptions."

CHAPTER 5

Dusting for Prints

"Today we're going to experiment with 10 things that are uniquely yours," Mr. Flask began just after the bell rang. "All you need is paper, a soft-lead pencil, and the tips of your fingers." He handed Alberta a box of number-one pencils to pass out.

"Take a look at your right thumb," Mr. Flask continued. "See the pattern of ridges that swirl around it? That pattern was the same when you were born, only smaller. It will look the same when you're 99, only bigger, and probably a bit wrinkled. What's more, none of the other six billion people in the world has the same —"

Suddenly, the door swung open.

"Detective Shapiro?" Mr. Flask looked confused.

"Uh-oh," Prescott whispered to Luis and Alberta.

"Come on in," the teacher continued. "I just wasn't expecting —"

"No, you weren't," the detective agreed. His gaze swept the room. "I'm here on official business. I'm afraid a crime has been committed. A string of thefts, perpetrated during my Community Safety Day presentation."

"My Walkman!" Heather blurted out.

"Yes, and nine other items from all over the school," the detective replied. "Since an item was stolen from this classroom, I'm going to have to dust for fingerprints."

"We were just studying fingerprints," Alberta said.

"Oh?" Detective Shapiro asked.

"Yes, as part of our detective science unit," Mr. Flask explained.

"Great," the detective said, "then I'd be happy to demonstrate by fingerprinting you right now."

Mr. Flask looked startled. "Oh! Okay." He thought for a moment, then smiled at the class. "It'll be interesting to compare a professional's technique with our classroom method."

After Detective Shapiro finished laying out some equipment, he poured a liquid onto a cloth and reached for Mr. Flask's hand. "First, I clean the fingers. Next, I help the suspect roll the tip of one finger over an ink pad. Then, I help him roll his inky fingertip over a special card." He held up the card. It had 10 boxes on it, one with a fresh print inside. "When I finish all 10, I have a record of the suspect's fingerprints, with the ridges marked in gray and the spaces between them in white."

Mr. Flask spoke up. "While the detective is working, use your soft-lead pencil to make a dark, powdery mark on a scrap of paper. Rub your index finger on the mark until you pick up a good coating of the black powder. Then carefully press your finger onto a clean piece of paper."

"Cool!" Sean said. "My fingerprint is black and orange — pencil dust and cheese-puff powder."

Mr. Flask laughed. "Go ahead and do all 10 fingers. Be careful — the prints can smudge. And don't forget to label which is which."

"But Mr. Fla-ask!" Max whined. "Now my fingers are dirty."

"When you're done, you can wash your hands." Mr. Flask stood up, waving his inky fingers. "Which I'll do now — with your permission, Detective."

Detective Shapiro nodded. "After I have a record of a suspect's prints, I can check them against *latent* fingerprints — the invisible prints we leave each time we touch something."

"If they're invisible, how can you find them?" Prescott asked.

The detective held up a small jar of black powder and a fluffy brush. "I'm going to *develop* them — or make them visible — using these."

Mr. Flask returned to the front of the classroom. The detective held out a paper bag. "Mr. Flask, could you take the drinking glass out of this bag and place it on your desk?"

Mr. Flask reached into the bag.

"Even though your teacher only touched the glass briefly," the detective continued, "he left behind fingerprints."

Mr. Flask smiled. "The prints are made of stuff we don't even realize we have on our fingers, like body oils and salty sweat."

Max looked at his fingers. "Ugh! I thought mucus was disgusting. But at least it was *inside* my body."

Detective Shapiro dipped his brush in the black powder and gently coated the outside of the glass. He blew away some excess powder. Then he carried the glass around the classroom.

"If every criminal left full, clear prints like these," he said, "a detective's job would be a cinch. Often, we can only find partial prints. But even then, we can make a match if we have the full prints on file."

Professor von Offel beckoned the detective back to his desk. He squinted at the prints. "You say you can trace these fingerprints back to any suspect?"

"If I have the prints on file," Detective Shapiro said.

"Can you pick fingerprints off of any surface?" the professor asked.

"For the method I just showed you, smooth, hard surfaces like glass or polished wood work best," the detective said. "But these days, big police departments have lasers and other high-tech fingerprinting equipment. They can develop prints on trickier surfaces, like plastic bags, rubber bands, or paper tissues."

"But here in Arcana, you don't have those new-fangled methods?" the professor asked.

The detective shook his head. "I could probably borrow some equipment if there was a serious crime here. But I can't haul in a laser just to find out who stole a Barbie doll." He returned to the front of the classroom and pulled out a piece of clear tape. "Now I'll just use this to pick up one of the prints." He pressed the tape to the glass, then removed it and stuck it on a piece of paper. He handed the paper to Luis, along with Mr. Flask's fingerprint card. "Does it match one of the prints?"

Luis scanned the two cards and nodded. "The right index finger."

Detective Shapiro carried the black powder and the brush back to Heather's desk. "This isn't ideal, since the crime scene has been disturbed. But I still might pick up something interesting." He signaled for Heather to move, then dusted the top of her desk. The students gathered around. Edgar wandered from one to another, sniffing and licking hands. After a few minutes' work, Detective Shapiro had five fingerprints. He compared them to Heather's paper.

"Four of these are yours," he said. He picked up the card with Mr. Flask's prints. After a moment he added, "Looks like the fifth one belongs to Mr. Flask." He turned toward the teacher.

Alberta made a face. "Of course, you're going to find Mr. Flask's prints in here! It's his classroom!"

The detective didn't reply. He was studying Heather's desk. "There are some other interesting marks here. I can't tell what they are, though." The class leaned closer. Edgar edged his way in and ran his nose along the top edge of the desk. He got a whiff of the black powder and sneezed.

Luis pointed to a fresh mark left by Edgar's nose. "Those on the other side must be dog-nose prints, too."

The detective nodded. "That doesn't explain these in the middle." He pointed to some marks that looked like lopsided X's.

The professor had been peering over the students' shoulders. When he saw the marks, he turned to Atom and lifted up one of his scaly feet. Two toes pointed forward and two pointed back, making an uneven X.

The parrot shrugged. "That Heather would be a babe in any species," he whispered. "You know what a flirt I am."

A few hours later, Alberta, Luis, and Prescott were filing out of the school building.

"I can't believe Detective Shapiro suspects Mr. Flask of stealing lemon Jell-O and a Barbie doll," Alberta said.

Prescott shook his head angrily. "Well, he hasn't exactly proven himself to be a brilliant detective. I mean, he spends three days in the same classroom with a ghost, and he doesn't even notice anything strange?"

"I have my own theory," Luis said quietly. "But I'm not sure it makes any sense. And I don't think things would be any better for Mr. Flask if it's true."

"We're waiting," Alberta prompted.

"Well, we already know there's one thief of sorts in Mr. Flask's classroom," Luis said.

"Edgar?" Alberta asked. "But how did he get inside Heather's backpack? And into the kindergarten coat closet? And into the woodshop cabinets? And the fridge in the cafeteria?"

Luis shrugged. "I told you it didn't make much sense. It just seems like it would be such a coincidence to have two different thieves come to school in the same week."

"Well, don't call Edgar a thief in front of Detective Shapiro," Alberta said. "He'd take him to the dog pound or something, and Mr. Flask would get in trouble anyway."

"Agreed." Luis grimaced. "Anyway, Mr. Flask still hasn't been charged with anything. I guess we just better keep our eyes open."

Mr. Klumpp crouched in the bushes outside the science lab. He checked his watch — almost three hours of misery so far and nothing to show for it. His legs were falling asleep. He had an itch in the middle of his back that he couldn't reach. And his hot, sweaty forehead kept fogging up his binoculars. The custodian wiped them on his shirt for the 50th time. "Surveillance work isn't for sissies," he reminded himself. He gritted his teeth and focused the binoculars on the lone figure of Mr. Flask. Through the window, the teacher appeared to be doing nothing more interesting than wiping off some desks. "Well, I'd better call it quits for today," the custodian said. "I'll catch him off guard tomorrow, though."

Mr. Klumpp put one hand on the ground and began to push himself to a standing position. The hand sank a few inches into the dirt and touched something hard. Mr. Klumpp put down his binoculars and pulled a small trowel from his tool belt. He carefully unearthed a glass disk circled in gold metal. "Buried treasure, eh? Maybe Dr. Kepler was telling the truth about the thefts — which means there's more to Flask's mischief than meets the eye." When he sprang up, he was a new man, full of energy.

A minute later, he stormed into the science lab.

"So, Flask, hiding your ill-gotten booty right under the nose of the authorities?" He waved the professor's monocle at the teacher.

"Excuse me?" Mr. Flask focused on the swinging disk. "Mr. Klumpp, you found the professor's monocle!" He held out a hand.

Mr. Klumpp snatched the disk away. "Not so fast. Why should I give this to you?"

Mr. Flask smiled. "Give it to the professor yourself. I'm just so relieved you found it. I felt awful when Edgar took off with it. It doesn't look that easy to replace."

The custodian scowled. "You're saying that your dog stole it?"

"You could say that, I guess," Mr. Flask said. "He has this awful habit of burying —"

"That makes it stolen property," Mr. Klumpp interrupted. "Don't you think I should turn it in to the police? Or is that too law-abiding for you?"

Mr. Flask laughed uncertainly. "It just seems a bit much. Edgar is only a dog, after all."

"Like to play fast and loose with the law, do you?" Mr. Klumpp said.

Mr. Flask flicked his thumb toward his skateboard, which was leaning against the wall. "Only the laws of physics," he joked.

The custodian scowled.

Mr. Flask sighed. "By all means, take the monocle to Detective Shapiro. He's probably somewhere in the building, dusting for fingerprints."

Mr. Klumpp turned on his heel and headed out the door.

Mr. Flask went back to wiping black powder off the windowsill. "*My* fingerprints," he added quietly.

Over in the principal's office, Detective Shapiro was pacing back and forth. "I'm closing in on Ethan

41

Flask," he said. "His fingerprints are all over the building."

Dr. Kepler took a deep breath. "As I explained yesterday, Ethan Flask has a valid reason to be all over the building. At my request, he's been helping other teachers incorporate science into their lessons."

Detective Shapiro made a face. "The kindergarten teacher, too? I found his prints all over the classroom where the Barbie doll was stolen."

"They're doing a unit on dairy farms," Dr. Kepler explained. "Ethan taught them about freezing and melting by having them make ice cream."

"Well, there are no teachers who need his help in the cafeteria kitchen," the detective countered. "Yet Flask's prints were all over the fridge that the gelatin mold was stolen from."

"He was probably keeping heavy cream in there, to make the ice cream," the principal said. "I bet you'd find his prints on the freezer, too, where he kept the ice."

The detective crossed his arms. "All for making ice cream, huh? I suppose he went into the wood shop for sawdust to give it that hickory-smoked flavor? Well? His prints were on the tool cabinet that held the stolen drill."

Dr. Kepler smiled. "Mr. Flask's ice cream–making technique calls for crushed ice. He lets the kids crush it themselves, using hammers from the wood shop."

Detective Shapiro sat down wearily. "I'm only

interested in justice, Dr. Kepler. I know you want to find this thief as much as I do."

The principal nodded.

"Then you have to be willing to look at this objectively. You may not know Ethan Flask as well as you think you do. Some criminals are very charming. On the outside, he seems like a very nice guy. But as we learned in detective school, things aren't always as they seem."

"Agreed," Dr. Kepler said. "But they often *are* as they seem."

"A good point," the detective said. "And right now it *seems* as though Ethan Flask is our thief. He's the only person who left the Community Safety Day presentation at any time."

"Maybe someone else entered the building?" the principal suggested.

"The school secretary says she didn't see anyone," Detective Shapiro said. "Do you have any reason to doubt her?"

"Of course not," Dr. Kepler said. "But perhaps someone came through a back door?"

"They were all locked," the detective replied.

"Or climbed in an open window?" Dr. Kepler suggested.

"Naturally, I checked the yard for unusual footprints," Detective Shapiro said. "There were none under any of the windows. Mostly, I found kids' footprints from recess. Plus mine — and those of Flask's dog."

Dr. Kepler thought for a moment. "This is an awful thought, but maybe someone came in earlier, hid in a closet, and snuck out during your presentation."

"I suppose that's possible," the detective said. "But it's not very probable. One of the boring secrets of detective work is this: The simplest explanation is usually the right one. And as of now, the simplest explanation is that your thief is Ethan Flask."

CHAPTER 6

None, Zippo, Zilch

"I heard Detective Shapiro dusted practically the whole school for fingerprints yesterday." Prescott followed the other two lab assistants into the lunchroom.

Alberta nodded. "Here's what I overheard in the office this morning: Detective Shapiro found Mr. Flask's fingerprints at a lot of the crime scenes. Dr. Kepler says all the prints can be explained, and she wants Detective Shapiro to look for other suspects. But Mrs. Ratner has been calling the police station, demanding that they solve this case right away. So Detective Shapiro is focusing all of his attention on Mr. Flask, because the detective insists he's the most likely suspect."

"Doesn't it seem like the police should take Dr. Kepler's word about Mr. Flask?" Prescott said. "It is her school."

Luis opened his lunch bag. "I have a new theory," he said. He took a bite of his sandwich and chewed slowly.

Alberta and Prescott watched impatiently.

"What is it with you and the suspense?" Prescott asked. "Tell us!"

"Well, what if these stolen objects have something to do with Professor von Offel?" Luis said. "A lot of strange things have happened since he came. Maybe this is just the latest."

"I like it," Alberta said. "Now that you mention it, I didn't see the professor at the Community Safety Day presentation at all. I guess nobody noticed, because he's not an official part of the staff. So he practically had the whole school to himself for about 45 minutes."

"That's plenty of time for him to have gathered those things and made them disappear in some freak science experiment or something," Prescott said.

Alberta frowned. "But how are we going to prove it to Detective Shapiro? He didn't find any of the professor's fingerprints in his search."

"He's a ghost, remember?" Prescott said. "He doesn't cast a shadow, so he probably doesn't leave fingerprints, either."

"I'm not convinced he's a ghost," Alberta said. "But maybe there's another reason Detective Shapiro didn't find the professor's fingerprints. Like, maybe he's found a scientific way to avoid leaving them."

"The first thing we should do is establish whether the professor leaves fingerprints," Luis said. "If we eat quickly, I think we can find out before lunch period ends."

Ten minutes later, the three lab assistants were sneaking into the empty lab.

Alberta hesitated by the door. "I feel funny about this," she said.

"Mr. Flask never said we couldn't visit the lab when he wasn't here," Prescott reasoned. He approached Professor von Offel's desk. "How about dusting the professor's teacup? You saw how easily Mr. Flask left prints by touching a drinking glass for just a second."

Luis nodded. "A lot of the dusting powder left over from yesterday is still in the garbage can. I bet I can gather enough to cover the cup."

"We need a way to brush it on," Alberta said. "I think I saw some soft paintbrushes in the cabinet."

A few minutes later, the three were studying the dusted teacup with magnifying lenses.

"Completely print-free," Prescott said. "Now do you believe me that he's a ghost?"

Just then, the door swung open and Edgar bounded in, with Mr. Flask behind. Edgar raced over to the professor's desk, scattering the lab assistants. He grabbed the teacup and dashed out the door.

"Edgar! Come back, boy!" Mr. Flask shouted down the hallway. The dog disappeared from sight. The teacher shook his head. "Back to square one."

Then he turned to the lab assistants. "What are you three doing here?" he demanded. "You can't hang around an empty classroom during lunchtime. Especially not while there's a police investigation going on!"

Prescott blushed. "Well, you never said we couldn't come in here at lunch."

Mr. Flask looked at Prescott for a long moment. "I hope you're joking."

Prescott smiled weakly. "Well, it did sound more convincing a few minutes ago."

Mr. Flask laughed. Then he shook his head. "I'm sorry, guys. But this police investigation is serious business."

"Actually, we were trying to help with the investigation," Alberta said. "That is —"

"We dusted the professor's teacup for fingerprints," Luis explained.

"And there weren't *any*," Prescott continued. "None, zippo, zilch. Which isn't possible — unless he's a ghost."

Mr. Flask shook his head. "I expect more scientific thinking from my lab assistants. You know there's no such thing as a ghost. There must be some simple explanation. Maybe the cup was freshly washed."

"But there was a tea stain inside," Prescott objected.

Mr. Flask held up a hand to stop him. "Here's the bottom line. There's a thief loose in this school. If

48

you three are caught sneaking around during lunch, someone is going to suspect *you*." He sighed. "Haven't we had enough wrongful insinuations in the last couple of days?"

Mr. Flask still seemed on edge when the rest of the sixth graders returned for science class.

The bell rang. "Sometimes, detectives need to see without being seen," Mr. Flask began, looking nervously at the door. He held up a long cardboard box with a mirror set into each end. "A periscope uses two mirrors to give you a new view."

Sean rubbed his hands together. "I can think of all kinds of uses for that baby," he laughed.

Mr. Flask bristled. "If I hear of anyone using these periscopes irresponsibly, you'll sit out science labs for a week!"

Sean held up his hands in mock surrender. "A joke, Mr. Flask!"

Mr. Flask's eyes flicked over to the door again. "Good," he said.

"Why does he keep looking at the door?" Alberta whispered to Luis.

On cue, the door swung open, and Detective Shapiro strode in. "I guess you're not surprised to see me, Flask," he said.

Mr. Flask forced a smile. "We should give you permanent guest speaker status."

"I'm not here to speak to your class today," the detective said. "I'm here for you."

"Are you going to handcuff him?" Sean asked.

"I'm not making any arrests — today," the detective said. "I just need to ask your teacher about this." He pulled a clear plastic bag out of his pocket. Inside was a wire-rimmed glass disk.

"The professor's monocle," Alberta said.

"So I've been told," the detective said grimly. He turned to Mr. Flask. "The custodian says you urged him to give this to me. Told him it belonged to Professor von Offel."

Mr. Flask nodded cautiously. "I didn't exactly *urge* him."

"Well, I tested this monocle myself," the detective replied. "It has an acid stain on it that *appears* to date back more than a hundred years. That's impossible, so obviously someone has been tampering with this evidence."

Mr. Flask opened his mouth to speak, then closed it again.

"Mr. Klumpp says he found this in the bushes right outside your window," the detective continued. "I can't help but suspect that *someone* planted it there just to throw off my investigation."

"This has spiraled way out of control," Mr. Flask said. "There's a simple explanation. My dog, Edgar, grabbed the professor's monocle and ran outside with it. I'm sure you won't find that hard to believe."

The detective made a face.

"He must have buried it under those bushes, where Mr. Klumpp found it," the teacher continued. "Now, what Mr. Klumpp was doing in the bushes —"

"What's unusual about a custodian cleaning under the bushes?" the detective asked. "Sounds like part of his job."

"Let me see that, Detective." The professor reached for the plastic bag. He turned it over in his hand. "Oh, that's not my monocle. Mine is of a much more modern design. Didn't you say you had one like that, Flask?"

Mr. Flask stared at the professor in amazement. The detective turned back to the teacher. "I see," he said. "Well, I'm going to have to ask you to come down to the station after school today. I'm sure we can get to the bottom of this if we try."

"All right," Mr. Flask said wearily.

"Just one more thing," the detective said. "I'm going to bring in a professional police dog to sniff around here. I'll need you to restrain your retriever while he's in here."

Mr. Flask tied up Edgar while Detective Shapiro brought in a large German shepherd.

"Harry here has a highly trained nose," the detective said. "He spent this morning sniffing the other nine crime scenes, like the wood shop and the kindergarten classroom. I admit that the trail is kind of cold by now. But I think this is worth a shot."

The detective led Harry over to Mr. Flask. The shepherd eagerly sniffed his pocket.

"Oh, Edgar's dog treats." Mr. Flask pulled one out of his pocket. "May I?"

Detective Shapiro looked annoyed, but he nodded. Across the room, Edgar whimpered.

Harry dutifully sniffed around the rest of the classroom. When he reached the professor's desk, the hair on the back of his neck bristled. He growled at Atom, then started barking wildly. The professor snatched the parrot from his perch and glared at the snarling police dog.

Detective Shapiro threw all of his weight into holding Harry back. "I don't understand it. This is a *professionally trained* dog."

"Well, he's obviously snapped," the professor shouted over the noise. "Clearly this simple parrot could have nothing to do with this ugly, complicated affair!"

It took the detective a full minute to drag the barking Harry to the door.

Mr. Flask followed him into the hallway. "Don't be too hard on Harry," he said. "The professor's bird often provokes that kind of response in other animals."

The detective narrowed his eyes. "I'll see *you* down at the station."

After class, Professor von Offel rushed to his office with Atom. He dropped the bird onto the desk and jabbed a finger at his beak.

"I'm going to *assume* that that police dog was just barking for a plateful of parrot à la king," the professor said. "Because if I find out that you were involved in this thievery, I may just serve him some."

"Of course, heh-heh, naturally!" Atom took a few steps back. "Purely out of curiosity, though, what do you have against whoever stole all those things?"

"Ethan Flask is not excused until he's helped me bring myself fully back to life!" the professor said. "It was one thing for him to take the blame for my . . . minor mishaps. But it's another for him to be hauled off to prison for an actual crime. If someone *must* be arrested, better him than me, but Flask is no good to me if he's in jail!"

Atom gulped. "I see."

"I'm not finished! Now, not only do I have to worry about losing Flask, I have to redirect some of my precious creative energy. The cranial power I could have spent bringing myself back to life must instead be wasted on shifting the blame away from Flask. Now, that's what I call a crime. But I might as well begin." The professor sat down at his desk and began riffling through his quill-written notes.

Atom fluttered over to his shoulder. "Well, if there's one thing you have in unlimited supply, it's creative energy. I've never seen anyone so — creative — when it comes to science theory."

"Flattery will get you nowhere," the professor sniffed. "But I'll accept your comments as unbiased observation."

Hours later, Mr. Flask stumbled out of the sheriff's office, rubbing his temples.

The lab assistants were waiting for him.

"What did they do to you?" Alberta asked. "You look awful!"

Luis jabbed Alberta's ribs with his elbow. "You just look a little tired, that's all. Did you get through to him?"

Mr. Flask shrugged. "I'm not sure. He let me go, but I think I'm still his number-one suspect."

"But if detectives are so much like scientists, why can't he use logic to see the truth — that you're innocent?" Alberta asked.

"He thinks he is being logical," Mr. Flask said. "All the evidence he has so far seems to point to me. He saw me leave the gymnasium during his presentation. He found my fingerprints at the crime scenes."

"It sounds like he needs different evidence," Prescott said.

Mr. Flask nodded. "He's going to come back tomorrow and search the school one more time. I'll be surprised if he finds anything new, though. He's been over it all before."

"Well, obviously he's looking in the wrong places," Prescott said.

Mr. Flask smiled. "Oh? Where do you think he should look?"

"In the gho — in the professor's office," Prescott answered.

Mr. Flask laughed. "You think Professor von Offel stole a Barbie doll and a Walkman?"

"Is that any stranger than his sliming the weight room?" Luis asked. "Or exploding a giant watermelon?"

"I admit he might be involved in that other mischief." Mr. Flask's face grew serious. "But I can't believe he'd steal from students or from the school. Where's your evidence?"

"Well, he wasn't at the Community Safety Day presentation, either," Luis said.

"Plus he's been trying to shift blame away from himself practically from day one," Prescott said. "Remember what he said during the lie detector test?"

"But according to the polygraph, he believed what he said." Mr. Flask thought for a moment. "Of course, that's different from it being right. So he was being truthful, but wrong."

"Does a lie detector test even work on a ghost?" Prescott asked.

"I've already said my piece on your ghost theory," Mr. Flask said.

"What about when Detective Shapiro brought in the professor's monocle today?" Alberta said. "The professor claimed it wasn't his! Like there could be two people at Einstein Elementary with monocles?"

"That *was* kind of strange," Mr. Flask admitted. "But none of those things prove anything, except that the professor is a bit eccentric, which we knew. He's a von Offel, after all."

"But if we don't tell the detective about the professor, he'll keep investigating you!" Alberta said.

Mr. Flask let out an exasperated sigh. "That's enough for tonight. I have to go pick up Edgar, anyway. Dr. Kepler was nice enough to take care of him this afternoon." Mr. Flask shook his head. "The first thing Edgar did when she took him outside was make a grab for her car keys. She wrestled them away, but that was a near disaster. I better get over to her house and see if he left anything unburied."

He smiled at his joke, but the lab assistants were all looking down quietly.

"Thanks for meeting me here," Mr. Flask added. "I needed to see some friendly faces. I'll catch you guys in class tomorrow."

Prescott shook his head. "It's Field Day tomorrow, remember? Classes are canceled."

Mr. Flask grinned. "That's right. You're looking at the referee for the three-legged race."

CHAPTER 7

Sneaking Around

" I don't have a great feeling about this," Prescott said. "What if they miss us out there?" He motioned across the empty science lab toward the view of the school yard. Hundreds of students were assembling for Field Day.

Luis was busy examining the professor's quill and inkwell. "Weren't you the one who told us 'But Mr. Flask never said we couldn't visit the lab without him'?"

"Yeah," Prescott said. "But that was before he *did* tell us we couldn't visit the lab without him."

Alberta poked her head out from under the professor's desk. "We're all nervous about this, but there's no other way. If we don't give Detective Shapiro some evidence on the professor, he's going to arrest Mr. Flask."

"As long as you can see that Mr. Flask is out in the school yard, we're safe," Luis reasoned.

"Oh, yeah." Prescott turned back toward the window. "He's out there with Edgar — somewhere. I'll find him again in a moment."

The door swung open, and Edgar trotted in.

Alberta quickly scooted out from under the professor's desk. "Mr. Flask!" she said. "There you are. I had an idea for a Field Day event, but I couldn't find you outside. So I came in here."

Mr. Flask raised his eyebrows suspiciously. "Oh? But I'm not coordinating the Field Day."

"I know, but it involves science equipment." Alberta glanced around.

"The periscopes we made yesterday," Prescott spoke up. "For — a periscope race."

"You're going to run around holding periscopes?" Mr. Flask asked. "That doesn't sound very safe."

"I said I'd help her work the bugs out of the idea," Luis said. "So if we can just take the periscopes now —"

Mr. Flask nodded. "Certainly. After all, if you're outside in the school yard perfecting periscope races, then there's no chance Detective Shapiro will catch you sneaking around in the school building."

"But —" Alberta began.

"So by all means take your periscopes outside," the teacher continued. "It'll make it easier for me to pick you out of the crowd — and track your progress."

"But —"

Luis cut Alberta off. "Of course, Mr. Flask. See you outside!"

The three grabbed their periscopes off the back counter and filed out into the hallway.

"That's it?" Alberta whispered. "We're going to give up that easily?

"No way," Luis whispered back. He turned around and waved at Mr. Flask, who was watching them from the doorway. Then he led the lab assistants outside. "Let's split up for a while. That'll make it harder for Mr. Flask to see us. He's supposed to referee the three-legged race in 20 minutes. So I'll meet you in the professor's office in 21 minutes, okay?"

Alberta and Prescott nodded.

Meanwhile, Dr. Kepler was closing her office door. She sat down behind her desk and faced Detective Shapiro.

"I've hesitated to say anything about Professor von Offel," Dr. Kepler began. "He is a guest here, after all. But in fairness to Ethan Flask, I feel I have to." She paused, thinking.

The detective frowned. "If you have any evidence linking the professor to these thefts, it's your duty to inform the police — even if he is a guest."

Dr. Kepler shook her head. "I don't have any direct evidence. It's just that we've had some very unusual — unexplained — events since he came."

"So I've heard," Detective Shapiro said. "But you haven't filed any crime reports, so I assume none of these events have been criminal."

"Not criminal," Dr. Kepler said slowly. "But in each case, there's no doubt that somebody was breaking the rules. It's just that it would be a bit hard to put your finger on *which* rules they were breaking."

The detective nodded. "Who would think to make up a rule about exploding watermelons?"

"Exactly," Dr. Kepler said. "Clearly, you've heard the stories. But what you don't know is that Ethan Flask and I have both noticed that the professor seems to be at the center of each of these incidents."

"Flask noticed this?" the detective asked. "That's interesting, because your custodian has also been observing carefully, and he believes *Flask* is responsible."

Dr. Kepler took a deep breath. "Mr. Klumpp is an excellent custodian. But I'm not sure he's an equally good detective. In my experience, he judges people mostly on the basis of how much mess they make." The principal smiled. "He even keeps me on my toes."

Detective Shapiro stood up. "I'll keep your concerns about the professor in mind. I assume you're giving me permission to search his office?"

Dr. Kepler sighed. "Let's just say you have permission to look anywhere in the school. My main concern is that you find evidence clearing Ethan Flask's name."

"I would think you'd want evidence leading to the truth," the detective said.

"I do," the principal insisted. "It's the same thing."

Professor von Offel was leading Atom down the empty hallway. Under his arm was a long metal tube the size and shape of a small cannon barrel.

The professor pushed open the door to the basement stairs. "As much as I hate to help a Flask, this should still be rather enjoyable."

Atom looked at the contraption under the professor's arm. "You're not going to shoot anyone with that, are you? You saw how easily that detective picks up fingerprints."

"That's what I'm counting on," the professor replied.

"Well, aren't your prints all over the outside of that gun?" Atom asked.

The professor looked at his hand. "I doubt I leave fingerprints. But in any case, it's more important whose prints are *inside* this gun, as you call it. That's why we're going to the custodian's workshop."

"Am I supposed to follow that logic?" Atom asked.

"I'll spell it out," the professor said. "In order to keep young Flask out of jail, we need to give Detective Shapiro a new suspect. I've picked the perfect candidate — that irritating custodian, Mr. Klumpp. Now all we need is some evidence."

"But if Klumpp isn't really guilty, how are you going to find any evidence in his workshop?" Atom asked.

"Why bother looking for evidence when you can make some up?" the professor scoffed. He pointed to the tube under his arm. "That's where my brilliant new invention comes in. All we need is a small item, like a tool, with Klumpp's fingerprint on it. I drop it into this chamber where a light beam reads the print pattern. Then when I aim at a surface and press the trigger, a nozzle projects an oily copy of Klumpp's fingerprint. Later, when Shapiro dusts the surface for prints, he finds solid evidence condemning Klumpp."

The professor opened the door to the custodian's workshop and flipped on the light.

"Help, I'm blinded!" squawked Atom. He fluttered unsteadily to the ground, eyes shut tight. Then he carefully opened one eye. "These tools are as shiny as mirrors. I haven't seen so much polished metal since your granddaughter Esmerelda made the world's largest solar cooker and got the world's fastest sunburn."

"Klumpp does keep his tools spotless," the professor agreed. "Let's just hope he couldn't polish off all the fingerprints." He pulled out a can of crystals and a Bunsen burner. He lit the burner under the crystals and stood back. The room began to fill with violet fumes.

Atom coughed. "That stuff smells toxic."

The professor nodded cheerfully. "Toxic *and* corrosive."

After a moment, the outlines of fingerprints showed up on a few scattered tools.

"Disappointingly few prints," the professor said. "But then we need only one." He picked up a hammer and placed it inside his invention. "Let's get to work."

Atom followed the professor out of the workshop. "Shouldn't we do something about those fumes? Seems like a health hazard for the custodian."

The professor shrugged. "If he's light-headed and dizzy, he'll be that much more believable as a suspect."

"Don't you have any respect for human life?" Atom asked.

"Of course I do," the professor replied. "Why do you think I'm trying so hard to become a hundred percent corporeal?"

"I meant respect for anyone *else*'s human life."

The professor looked puzzled. "Like whose?"

Atom shook his head. "Forget I asked."

Meanwhile, Prescott was kneeling in the professor's office and holding up two handfuls of paper. "That's all there is in the professor's desk. Just stacks and stacks of notes. I can't even read them. The writing is too old-fashioned."

Alberta reached for a page. "I might be able to decipher them. I had a lot of practice with Johannes von Offel's science notebooks." She studied the notes for a moment. "Actually, this writing looks a lot like Johannes's. I guess all old-fashioned writing looks similar."

Prescott looked over her shoulder. "This is more evidence that von Offel is a ghost. Nobody writes like that anymore."

Suddenly, Atom's shadow passed across the frosted-glass door.

Prescott's eyes widened. "The professor!"

"Into the closet!" Luis whispered. Prescott crammed the papers back into the desk and slid the drawers closed. Then all three folded themselves into the professor's tiny closet.

"I can't breathe!" Prescott whispered.

"Then don't," Luis replied.

They waited for three long, musty minutes.

"Must have been a false alarm," Alberta whispered.

Luis turned the handle on the closet door, and he and Alberta stumbled out. "I guess we better get out of here, though. Who knew the professor would come in on Field Day? Mr. Flask isn't even teaching today."

Prescott was still picking himself up off the closet floor. "Hey, what's that?" He pointed to a box on a high, half-hidden shelf.

Luis gave Prescott a boost, and he pulled it down. "Looks like a small, old-fashioned trunk."

Alberta opened some clasps on the side and swung open the lid. "What is this stuff?"

Prescott peered in. "These things belong in a museum. There's a buggy whip, a buttonhook, a warming pan . . ."

"Here's a stovepipe hat like the one President Lincoln wore," Alberta said.

Luis reached in. "Look at the old coins at the bottom. This one says 1876."

"Why does he have this stuff?" Alberta asked. "Could he have stolen it?"

Prescott shook his head. "Don't you get it? Not only is the professor a ghost, he's a ghost from the 1800s."

Alberta made a face.

"Shhh!" Luis whispered. "Footsteps."

CHAPTER 8

An Earth-shattering Conclusion

Alberta closed the lid of the trunk. Prescott and Luis slipped into the closet. Alberta tried to cram in with the trunk.

"Give me a boost, and I'll put it back," Prescott whispered.

A shadow fell across the frosted glass.

"Too late," Luis whispered.

The doorknob jiggled.

"Detective Shapiro!" Mr. Flask's voice rang from down the hall. "Could I interrupt your work for a minute?"

"If it's important," said the figure right outside the door.

"It — it might be," Mr. Flask said. "I'll let you be the judge. It's in the cafeteria."

The shadow disappeared. As soon as the footsteps faded, the lab assistants quickly returned the trunk and closed the closet door.

"Whew, that was close," Prescott said.

Suddenly, the office door swung open.

"When I didn't see you at the three-legged race, I knew I'd find you in there!" Mr. Flask whispered harshly. "Get out here!" He closed the office door behind them.

"But where's Detective Shapiro?" Prescott asked.

"In the cafeteria, waiting for me to show him some important evidence." Mr. Flask shook his head grimly. "I have no idea what I'm going to say to him. Obviously, I don't have any."

Prescott looked at Alberta and Luis. He cleared his throat. "We found some evidence. It's hidden in the professor's closet."

Mr. Flask's features grew a little more hopeful. "Some of the stolen objects?"

Prescott shook his head. "A whole trunkful of old-fashioned things, like a buggy whip and a stovepipe hat."

Mr. Flask's expression darkened.

"No one uses that kind of stuff anymore," Prescott explained. "So it's more proof that the professor is a ghost from more than a hundred —"

"Alberta and I thought maybe the stuff was stolen," Luis interrupted. "Maybe Detective Shapiro would know?"

Mr. Flask flushed with anger. "I'm pretty confident that no one at Einstein Elementary has reported missing any buggy whips!"

"Well, why does he have that stuff, then?" Prescott asked.

"People collect that kind of thing," Mr. Flask said.

"Remember, this is a man who wears a monocle and writes with a quill. Obviously, he likes antiques."

"Then why was he hiding them on a high shelf in his closet?" Alberta asked. "That seems pretty suspicious to me."

"Antiques are valuable," Mr. Flask said. "He probably wanted to keep them safe. There *have* been some thefts around here, remember?"

Alberta's face fell. "Oh, yeah."

"Now, I need all of you out of this building," Mr. Flask said. "I've got to figure out what to say to Detective Shapiro. Preferably something that won't make him suspect me even more."

The lab assistants started toward the door.

Luis stopped and looked back. "We're sorry, Mr. Flask. We only wanted to help."

"I know." The teacher sighed. "Please, just get outside and stay outside." He waited until the students were out of the building, then started down the hall toward the cafeteria.

When he turned the corner, he almost bumped into the professor. Atom squawked in surprise.

"Sorry, Professor."

"Flask."

Mr. Flask eyed the long metal tube under the professor's arm. "That looks interesting."

"Yes, it does," the professor agreed, walking on.

Mr. Flask watched the professor and his bird turn the corner. Should he follow?

"Flask! Are you coming?" Detective Shapiro poked his head out of the cafeteria. "Let's make this quick. They're cooking sloppy joes, and I'm not sure I can stand the smell for much longer."

A minute later, the professor and Atom slipped into a math classroom.

"First, we need a theft," the professor said. He approached the teacher's desk and lifted a calculator. "This will be missed right away. No math teacher can survive a day without using a calculator."

Atom hopped up on the desk. "What next?"

"Time to plant a few well-placed fingerprints," the professor said. "Did you bring the dusting powder? I don't usually waste time testing my inventions, but a man's honor hangs in the balance."

"Flask's honor?"

"No, Klumpp's. I've got to tarnish it."

Atom held up a brush in one claw. "I'm ready to dust. Fire away."

The professor aimed his invention at the desk. *Zap!* Atom flew over to check for a print.

"There's nothing here," Atom said. "I guess that's one more dastardly plan that doesn't work."

"Of course it works!" the professor said. "I just have to turn up the power. Stand back."

He twisted a knob on the side of his invention and aimed again.

Crash!

The window behind the desk shattered, as a blast of air knocked the professor backward and slammed Atom into the far wall.

The parrot slid to the floor, his vision swimming with stars. "Any chance you could recalibrate the recoil?" he asked.

When the cafeteria floor stopped shaking, Mr. Flask and Detective Shapiro staggered to their feet. A river of sloppy-joe mix flowed out of the kitchen and soaked the detective's shoes. He glanced down briefly and winced, then took off for the door. "Come with me, Flask," he ordered. "I may need help."

Outside, the school yard was crisscrossed with a tangled mass of six-foot trenches. Luis and Alberta struggled to pull Prescott up to level ground.

"Look at the goalposts," Prescott said. "They're twisted like giant metal pretzels."

Mr. Klumpp was running the system of trenches like a mouse in a maze. "Earthquake! Earthquake! Prepare for aftershocks!" he yelled.

The professor stroked his chin. He looked out the shattered window of the math classroom. "Fascinating. We seem to have projected a gargantuan replica of Klumpp's fingerprint into the ground itself."

Atom flew a little unsteadily to his perch on the professor's shoulder.

The professor looked at the bird disdainfully. "And you said it wouldn't work."

Back in the school yard, Mr. Flask and Detective Shapiro hauled students out of trenches and reunited them with teachers. Suddenly, there was a chorus of shouts a few trenches away. The teacher and the detective made their way over, the lab assistants right behind them. They all peered over the edge, expecting the worst.

"My Barbie! I found my Barbie!" a kindergartner screamed. She hugged the dirt-covered doll.

Luis pointed behind the girl. "That looks like Heather's Walkman."

"What kind of thief would steal stuff, just to bury it in the school yard?" Prescott asked.

Detective Shapiro jumped down into the valley and kicked the soil. "Here's the power drill and the Jell-O mold — empty, thank goodness." He lifted up something else.

"My microscope!" Mr. Flask said.

Detective Shapiro picked up a piece of notebook paper and brushed the dirt off it.

"My English homework!" Prescott reached for the paper. "Hmm, I wonder if neatness counts."

The detective kicked at the soil a little more and came up with his notebook. It was covered with teeth marks and paw prints. "I guess I don't need this anymore," he said. "The case is officially closed. I don't understand how, but clearly the dog did it."

Atom flew close to the broken window and shook his feathered head. "Look at that chaos out there. You've done it now. You think the cops were nosing around before? Now they'll be all over you like glaze on a donut."

The professor shrugged. "Relax. Our secret is safe. The only way you would ever know those trenches are a giant fingerprint is if you had a bird's-eye view from several hundred feet up. Luckily, there's no chance of that."

Whop-whop-whop-whop!

A traffic helicopter passed directly over the school yard.

The professor grabbed Atom by the legs. "You birdbrain, why didn't you tell me that humans have mastered flight?"

Welcome to the World of
MAD SCIENCE!

The Mad Science Group has been providing live, interactive, exciting science experiences for children throughout the world for more than 12 years. Our goal is to provide children with fun, entertaining, and exciting activities that instill a clearer understanding of what science is really about and how it affects the world around them. Founded in Montreal, Canada, we currently have 125 locations throughout the world.

Our commitment to science education is demonstrated throughout this imaginative series that mixes hilarious fiction with factual information to show how science plays an important role in our daily lives. To add to the learning fun, we've also created exciting, accessible experiment logs so that children can bring the excitement of hands-on science right into their homes.

To discover more about Mad Science and how to bring our interactive science experience to your home or school, check out our website:
http://www.madscience.org

We spark the imagination and curiosity of children everywhere!